A BOOK BY S AN

Predators

The Samurai X

Published by The Samurai X, 2024.

This is a work of fiction. Similarities to real people, places, or events are entirely coincidental.

PREDATORS

First edition. October 13, 2024.

Copyright © 2024 The Samurai X.

ISBN: 979-8230403326

Written by The Samurai X.

Table of Contents

Title Page 1

A B O U T 7

Chapter 1 | The Asteroid's Arrival 9

Chapter 4 The King 89

Post-Story Scene 121

Post-Story Scene 123

Post-Story Scene 125

"In the shadow of chaos, humanity's greatest strength is not in its weapons, but in its unyielding will to survive."

-by The Samurai

ABOUT

Title: *The Predators*
Series: *The Predators (Book 1)* **Author:** *The Samurai*
Genre: *Sci-Fi Thriller*

The Predators is the thrilling first installment in an electrifying new series by indie author The Samurai. This sci-fi thriller takes readers on a heart-pounding journey into a world where humanity's very survival is at stake.

When an asteroid crashes into Earth, it brings with it a deadly alien organism. These worms, once exposed to Earth's atmosphere, grow rapidly and evolve into terrifying predators. Capable of killing with a single touch and reproducing by planting eggs inside human hosts, these creatures soon become humanity's worst nightmare.

As the predators spread across the American continent, a group of scientists and survivors must navigate the chaos and find a way to fight back. Led by Emily and her parents, renowned scientists, they discover that the only way to stop the predators lies in the very asteroid that brought them here. Their journey to obtain a critical sample from the asteroid

Chapter 1
The Asteroid's Arrival

Cedar Falls was the kind of town that most people forgot existed. Tucked away in a remote valley surrounded by dense forests, it was quiet, picturesque even, with its small population of families and retirees living in blissful isolation. The townspeople enjoyed the tranquility, the predictability. Nothing ever seemed to happen in Cedar Falls—until that night.

It started out just like any other evening.

Parents were calling their kids in for dinner.

The local diner was buzzing with its usual small crowd of regulars. A football game was playing on TV, and people were half-watching, half-conversing, unaware of the celestial drama unfolding above them.

Chapter 1

At first, the flash in the sky seemed like a meteor shower—just one of those rare but awe-inspiring natural events. People looked up and marveled at the streaks of light cutting through the stars. But this wasn't an ordinary meteor.

The bright streak grew larger, the light intensifying until it seemed to fill the entire night sky, casting an eerie glow over the town.

As it came closer, there was a deafening roar, like thunder but far more violent. The ground trembled. Windows rattled. A few car alarms went off, as if nature itself was warning everyone to take cover. But before anyone could make sense of what was happening, the asteroid struck.

The impact was catastrophic, hitting the forest just outside of town with the force of a bomb. The ground shook violently, knocking dishes off shelves and sending anyone outside stumbling. Birds erupted from the treetops in frantic flocks, their cries lost beneath the roar. For a moment, the town was plunged into stunned silence.

Chapter 1

Then, as the initial shockwave passed, the

aftermath became all too clear. The once tranquil forest had been torn apart. Trees lay in splintered

ruins, smoke and ash rising from a massive crater in the earth. The eerie glow still emanated from the

impact zone, casting an unsettling light across the surrounding landscape.

Sheriff Hank Doyle was one of the first to respond. His phone had been ringing off the hook since the moment the asteroid hit. It felt surreal, like some

kind of apocalyptic movie. Hank wasn't used to this kind of thing. In Cedar Falls, his job mostly

involved chasing down stray dogs, breaking up the occasional bar fight, and dealing with speeding

tickets. An asteroid strike wasn't something he was prepared for.

He threw on his jacket, grabbed his keys, and

radioed for his deputy, Carl, to meet him at the crash site. By the time they pulled up near the forest, the fire department was already there,

attempting to put out the flames that had erupted in the surrounding trees.

Chapter 1

The scene was chaotic—firefighters dousing the scorched earth, townspeople gathering at a safe

distance, whispering nervously to one another. The glow from the asteroid cast strange, flickering

shadows across the landscape, making everything seem even more otherworldly. Hank's heart raced as he stepped out of his cruiser, looking at the

massive crater that had torn through the earth.

"What do you make of it, Sheriff?" Carl asked, staring wide-eyed at the scene.

"I don't know, but it sure as hell isn't just a

meteor," Hank muttered, his gaze fixed on the glowing rock at the center of the crater.

It wasn't like anything he had ever seen. The

asteroid was smooth, its surface almost metallic, and it pulsed faintly with an unsettling blue light.

Thin tendrils of vapor seeped from the cracks in its surface, snaking through the air and disappearing

into the night. As he watched, something else

caught Hank's eye—a strange movement near the rock's base.

Chapter 1

One of the firefighters, Kevin, had gotten closer to the asteroid than anyone else. He was crouched

near the edge of the crater, shining his flashlight onto the asteroid's surface, his face a mix of

curiosity and fear. Without warning, a strange black shape slithered out from the crevice. It was small,

no larger than a finger, but it moved with alarming speed, darting toward Kevin.

"What the hell...?" Kevin murmured, standing up quickly, but before he could react, the creature

lunged at him, wrapping itself around his wrist.

Kevin's scream echoed through the forest as the worm-like creature burrowed into his skin,

disappearing beneath the surface in seconds. He dropped his flashlight and fell to his knees,

clutching his arm in agony. The firefighters rushed to his side, but there was nothing they could do.

The strange creature had entered his body, and

whatever it was doing to him, it was happening fast.

Chapter 1

Everyone froze. Hank felt a cold chill run down his spine as he stared at Kevin's body, now still and

eerily silent. The thing—whatever it was—had killed him in moments.

"We need to get everyone out of here," Hank said, his voice hoarse. "Now."

But as he spoke, more movement caught his eye.

The ground around the asteroid began to stir as

more of the worm-like creatures slithered out from the cracks, their sleek, dark bodies moving with

terrifying speed.

"Get back!" Carl yelled, pulling Hank away as one of the creatures darted toward them. The firefighters scrambled, trying to pull Kevin's body away, but it was too late. The worms were spreading, slithering through the earth, heading for the town.

By the time Hank and Carl made it back to Cedar Falls, the situation had spiraled out of control.

People were running through the streets, panicking as news of the asteroid spread like wildfire. Some

had seen the strange creatures already—dark shapes moving too fast to identify, but leaving a trail of

death in their wake.

Chapter 1

EVERYONE FROZE. HANK felt a cold chill run down his spine as he stared at Kevin's body, now still and

eerily silent. The thing—whatever it was—had killed him in moments.

"We need to get everyone out of here," Hank said, his voice hoarse. "Now."

But as he spoke, more movement caught his eye.

The ground around the asteroid began to stir as

more of the worm-like creatures slithered out from the cracks, their sleek, dark bodies moving with

terrifying speed.

Chapter 1

Get back!" Carl yelled, pulling Hank away as one of the creatures darted toward them. The firefighters scrambled, trying to pull Kevin's body away, but it was too late. The worms were spreading, slithering through the earth, heading for the town.

By the time Hank and Carl made it back to Cedar Falls, the situation had spiraled out of control.

People were running through the streets, panicking as news of the asteroid spread like wildfire. Some

had seen the strange creatures already—dark shapes moving too fast to identify, but leaving a trail of

death in their wake.

Hank tried to maintain order, but the fear was

palpable. People were locking themselves inside their homes, barricading doors and windows,

unsure of what exactly they were hiding from. The phones at the sheriff's station were ringing off the hook, calls coming in from terrified residents

reporting strange sightings, deaths, and disappearing neighbors.

Chapter 1

That night, the predators made their first real attack on Cedar Falls. It started with isolated incidents—families torn apart in their homes,

people vanishing from the streets. The creatures had grown bold, breaking through windows,

crawling through cracks, and dragging their victims into the shadows.

Hank received the first call just after midnight. It came from a woman who lived on the outskirts of town, near the forest. She had seen the creatures earlier in the evening, lurking near her home, and

had barricaded herself inside with her husband and two young children. But the predators had found a way in.

When Hank and Carl arrived, the house was silent. The front door had been torn from its hinges, and the living room was a scene of unimaginable

carnage. Blood spattered the walls, furniture

overturned, the bodies of the woman and her family torn apart as if by some wild animal. But it wasn't

an animal that had done this. The claw marks on the walls, the jagged slashes through flesh and bone,

were far too deliberate for that

Chapter 1

THE ONLY SURVIVOR WAS the woman's son, a ten-year-old boy named Tommy, who had hidden in the

closet. He was shaking uncontrollably, his face pale with terror, unable to speak. Hank knelt beside him, his heart heavy with a sense of dread he couldn't

shake.

"What did you see?" Hank asked gently.

Tommy's voice was barely a whisper. "Monsters. They're monsters."

Chapter 1

The following morning, the sun rose over Cedar Falls, but the light felt muted, the air thick with tension. Sirens wailed as the remaining police

officers attempted to restore some semblance of

order, but chaos reigned. News of the asteroid strike and the subsequent attacks had spread

through town like wildfire, igniting a panic that no

one could contain.

Hank gathered the remaining deputies in the

station, urgency etched on their faces. He laid out a map of Cedar Falls, marked with the locations of the attacks, trying to create a plan.

"Look, we need to set up checkpoints," Hank said, his voice steady, masking the fear creeping in. "We can't let anyone out of town until we know what

we're dealing with. And we need to find the families that are still missing."

Carl, ever the pragmatist, nodded. "We should also set up a curfew. If people are out after dark, they're easy targets."

Chapter 1

As they discussed their strategy, the station's phone rang incessantly. Every call was from

terrified residents, pleading for help, recounting horrifying tales of the creatures that had invaded

their homes. Each story felt more unbelievable than the last, yet Hank knew they were all true.

As the day wore on, the situation grew increasingly dire. The town mayor, Evelyn Watts, arrived at the station, her expression one of grave concern. She

was flanked by two representatives from the state police, both looking equally frazzled.

"We need to take this seriously, Sheriff," Evelyn said, her voice a mixture of authority and fear.

"People are terrified. We can't let this escalate further. We need to coordinate with the state police, maybe even the National Guard."

Hank felt a wave of frustration. "They'll take too long to get here. We can't wait for backup. We have to act now."

Chapter 1

The state police officers exchanged glances. One of them, a tall man with a rugged face, spoke up. "We need to understand the situation first. Let's gather more information before we start making waves."

Before Hank could respond, the station was jolted by a loud crash outside. The windows rattled as

screams echoed through the streets. Without

hesitation, Hank and the others rushed out to see what had happened.

In the middle of the street stood a massive creature, one of the predators. It was unlike anything they

had encountered before. Its body was a grotesque fusion of dark, slick flesh and jagged, metallic

armor, glistening in the sunlight. Long, spindly

limbs ended in razor-sharp claws that dripped with a viscous, dark substance.

The creature was standing over a car, its jaws

unhinged and a hideous screech escaping its throat, echoing off the buildings like a siren of death. A

group of residents had gathered, frozen in shock,

and Hank realized they were mere feet away from a predator.

Chapter 1

GET BACK!" HANK SHOUTED, his heart racing. He

grabbed Carl and the others, ushering them toward the frightened crowd, trying to create a barrier

between them and the creature.

The predator's attention turned, its face fixating on them. It moved with a speed that was disconcerting, launching itself toward Hank and the others.

Without thinking, Hank drew his firearm, taking

aim, but a second later, a burst of gunfire erupted from the state police officers.

Chapter 1

The shots echoed through the town, each bullet striking the predator, but it barely flinched. It was as if the creature was impervious to the bullets, its body adapting even to this assault. With a swift, powerful movement, it swiped at the officers, sending one flying into the air like a rag doll.

Hank's instincts kicked in. "We need to retreat! Now!" he yelled, herding the townsfolk away from the horror unfolding before them.

As they backed away, the predator began to chase after them, its long limbs propelling it forward with terrifying grace. The air was thick with screams, panic rising as more people spilled into the streets, trying to escape the chaos.

Hank felt a surge of adrenaline as he fired again, aiming for the creature's center mass. This time, the shot struck true. The predator staggered back, letting out a horrific screech that sent chills down his spine. For a brief moment, it seemed stunned.

"Get to safety!" Hank shouted at the onlookers. "Now! Find shelter!"

Chapter 1

He turned to Carl, his breath heavy with urgency. "We need to regroup. Get everyone to the

community center—it's the safest place in town."

As they retreated, Hank caught a glimpse of the

predator regaining its composure. It bared its teeth, mouth wide, revealing rows of glistening, serrated

fangs. The creature was more than just a mindless monster; it was a predator in every sense of the

word, cunning and powerful.

Once they reached the community center, Hank and Carl helped to barricade the doors as quickly as

they could. The interior buzzed with terrified

chatter, people huddled together in fear, sharing

their own harrowing experiences. Parents held their children close, while the elderly whispered prayers, hoping for a miracle.

"We need to stay calm," Hank urged, his voice firm. "Help will be on the way. We're going to ride this

out together."

Chapter 1

The hours dragged on, each passing moment thick with tension. Reports from outside painted a grim picture: the predators were multiplying, and their attacks were becoming increasingly coordinated. It wasn't long before someone reported that one of

the nearby families hadn't made it to safety.

"Sarah and Mike are missing," a frantic woman

cried, her voice breaking. "They were at the diner when the asteroid hit. They never came home!"

A heavy silence fell over the group. Hank could feel the weight of despair settling in. They were losing people—families, friends, and neighbors. Each

moment they spent in fear only brought them closer to the inevitable.

Finally, Hank turned to the group, his voice steady despite the turmoil inside. "We need volunteers to check on other families. We can't wait here and do nothing."

A few brave souls stepped forward, determination etched on their faces. Among them was a young

woman named Emily, a recent college graduate studying biology. "I can help," she said.

Chapter 1

" My parents are scientist. They can help us out. I am sure that they are in their labs, in the old

research centre in the outskirts of the city, " Emily said, giving hope to everyone present there.

Hank nodded, grateful for her courage. "Okay, we'll form a small group and head out. But we need to

stay together and be cautious."

As they prepared to leave, Hank felt the weight of responsibility pressing down on him. He had to

keep his town safe, to protect the people he cared about. The creatures were out there, growing

stronger with each passing moment, and they had to find a way to fight back.

Chapter 2 The Evolution

As dawn broke over Cedar Falls, the streets lay eerily silent, punctuated only by the occasional distant screech of the predators prowling the

shadows. Hank, Emily, and a small group of

survivors moved with caution, eyes scanning every dark corner and alley. They were heading to the

outskirts of town, to the old research facility

where Emily's parents worked—her only hope in finding them alive.

Emily gripped her flashlight tightly, her mind

racing with fear and determination. Her parents, Dr. Samuel and Dr. Lillian Carter, were renowned scientists who had been working on experimental projects in bioengineering and ecology. She clung to the hope that they might still be at the facility,

sheltering from the nightmare unfolding across the town.

Chapter 2

Hank stayed close to her side, his eyes sharp and attentive. He had seen enough horror in the past

hours to know that their every step was dangerous. "Emily, we'll get them," he assured her. "Your

parents know how to survive."

Finally, they arrived at the research facility. The place was dark and deserted, but the doors were

intact, and there were signs of life inside. The group stepped in cautiously, closing the doors behind

them. In the distance, muffled sounds echoed down the hall—footsteps and the faint hum of machinery.

They moved deeper into the building, calling out as they went. Soon, a pair of familiar faces emerged

from a shadowed doorway: Dr. Samuel Carter, a tall man with salt-and-pepper hair, and Dr. Lillian

Carter, a slender woman with sharp eyes and a calm demeanor. They looked worn but unharmed.

"Emily!" Dr. Lillian cried, pulling her daughter into a tight embrace. "We thought—" She choked on her words, holding back tears. "We thought you didn't make it."

Chapter 2

"I'M HERE, MOM. I'M safe." Emily's relief was palpable, and for a moment, the horror of the past night faded. She turned to her father. "Dad, we need to find a way out. The creatures—they're everywhere. We can't stay here."

Dr. Samuel nodded, his face grim. "We've been monitoring their movement. They're spreading faster than anyone could've anticipated. This facility isn't secure for much longer."

Chapter 2

With renewed determination, the group, now

including Emily's parents, set off to the rendezvous point where a convoy of survivors was gathering.

The plan was to make their way to a remote

underground base, a secret facility built during the Cold War and recently refurbished by the

government for emergency use.

The journey was fraught with tension. At every

turn, they heard the chittering sounds of predators in the distance, their haunting screeches echoing

through the streets. Although the creatures avoided sunlight, they still lurked in dark alleys and

abandoned buildings, ready to attack at the slightest hint of weakness.

By evening, they finally reached the bunker. The

base was an imposing structure, hidden in the side of a mountain and fortified with thick metal doors and advanced surveillance systems. As they

descended into the underground chambers, the

survivors felt a semblance of safety. But the relief was short-lived.

Chapter 2

Inside the base, the halls were filled with other survivors—scientists, military personnel, government officials, and even a few wealthy civilians who had secured their spots. Despite the crowd, there was a sense of dread in the air.

Everyone knew they were just buying time.

That night, the survivors huddled in a large common room, listening to reports crackling through an old, battered radio. The voice on the other end was calm but strained, relaying news from other parts of the continent.

"Reports indicate predator sightings across major cities," the announcer's voice stated. "Washington D. C., New York, Los Angeles... the creatures are advancing. It appears they are expanding their territory rapidly, adapting to new environments with alarming speed."

Emily felt a chill run down her spine. The creatures weren't just an isolated threat—they were spreading, a plague covering the entire continent. Each new report drove home the horrifying reality: this was no longer a local disaster; it was an invasion.

Chapter 2

The announcer continued, "While the predators are faster and more aggressive at night, recent studies show they struggle to see in direct sunlight. The

creatures have developed a strange, multi-lensed eye structure, but it appears that their vision is

severely impaired during the day. At night, however... they are nearly unstoppable."

Emily's father leaned closer, muttering to himself. "The creatures have adapted rapidly. They've

evolved defenses and weaknesses in a matter of hours." He paused, thoughtful. "If only we could

find the source of these changes... perhaps we could

find a way to slow them down."

Emily watched her father closely, a flicker of hope rising within her. If anyone could figure out a way to fight back, it would be her parents.

Later that night, Dr. Samuel gathered Emily, Hank, and a few others to go over what he had learned

about the predators' biology. Using sketches and a few grisly photos from other survivors, he pieced together the anatomy of the creatures.

Chapter 2

"From what we've observed, the predators began as simple worm-like organisms—parasites, really," he

explained. "But once they found a host, they grew at an unprecedented rate, consuming flesh and

adapting traits. They're practically built for predation."

He held up a sketch showing the predator's

grotesque, elongated body, covered in thick, armor-like scales that shimmered with a metallic hue. Its

long limbs ended in clawed appendages, sharp as razors, capable of slicing through flesh and even some metals. And its face...

Chapter 2

Emily shuddered as she looked at the sketch of the predator's face. It had a strange, almost skeletal

structure, with hollowed cheekbones and a gaping mouth lined with rows of needle-like teeth. But the most unnerving feature was its eyes—bulbous,

multi-lensed orbs that seemed to stare into nothingness.

"These eyes," Dr. Samuel continued, pointing to the predator's face, "are complex, like those of an

insect. During the day, they're almost useless, but at night, they can see with perfect clarity, even in complete darkness. And they hunt in packs,

coordinating their attacks." The others listened in silence, each revelation deepening their horror.

"So they're blind in the day, but they hunt in packs at night?" Hank asked, frowning. "That means we

have a limited window to move safely."

"Exactly," Dr. Samuel confirmed. "Our best chance to escape or gather resources will be during the

day. But even then, we have to be careful. They're still dangerous—they rely on other senses when

their vision fails."

Chapter 2

The next morning, Emily and her parents joined a team of survivors who had volunteered to venture back to Cedar Falls. Their mission was simple:

gather supplies, monitor the creatures, and—if possible—collect samples of predator tissue for further research.

They moved through the ruined streets, every

sound putting them on edge. Even in the daylight, the predators lingered in the shadows, hissing

softly as they sensed the humans nearby. Emily gripped her father's hand tightly as they crept through an old grocery store, loading cans and medical supplies into backpacks as quickly and quietly as they could.

Just as they were about to leave, Emily spotted something near the entrance: a dark, viscous

substance trailing along the floor. She knelt, examining it closely.

"Is this... predator blood?" she asked, looking up at her father. Dr. Samuel nodded, his face alight with fascination and horror.

Chapter 2

He carefully collected a sample, sealing it in a container. "This could be what we need to

understand them better," he said, his voice a

whisper of hope. As the team made their way back

to the base, the radio crackled with another report. The announcer's voice was grim.

"Casualties continue to rise across the country.

Governments are struggling to control the spread, and evacuation efforts are ongoing. We are urging everyone to stay indoors and avoid any dark areas after nightfall."

Emily's heart sank. Even with her father's research, the predators were spreading faster than anyone

could have imagined. Cities were falling one by one, and humanity's hold on survival was slipping

through their fingers.

By the time they returned to the base, night had fallen, and the predators were already stirring in

the shadows outside. The survivors settled into the dim, claustrophobic halls, haunted by the grim

news and the reality of the monsters waiting outside.

Chapter 2

That night, Dr. Samuel and Dr. Lillian worked

tirelessly, analyzing the predator sample. They isolated its cells, studying its structure under a microscope, noting its incredible resilience and adaptability.

As they pored over the data, a realization struck

them. "It' s Origin," Dr. Lillian murmured. "We have to find it' s origin.... there might be something

there." Emily overheard her mother and felt a sliver of hope. But reaching the place that they were

unaware of, is dangerous.

In the days that followed their initial encounter with the predators, an unsettling truth became clear: these creatures were evolving far more

quickly than anyone could have anticipated. Back at the base, tension mounted as word spread that the

predators were now showing signs of resistance to firearms. Their bodies seemed to absorb bullets,

thickening their armored scales with each new encounter. Hank, who had always relied on his trusty shotgun, found himself grappling with a newfound helplessness.

Chapter 2

"We're running out of options," he murmured to

Emily, wiping sweat from his brow. "If bullets don't work, how are we supposed to keep them at bay?"

Emily, her face a mix of horror and determination, replied, "We'll have to find another way. Maybe my parents will come up with something... if we can

keep them safe long enough."

At the laboratory within the base, Dr. Samuel and

Dr. Lillian were frantically researching the predator sample they had collected. Days of relentless study revealed that the creatures' cells contained an

unparalleled adaptive mechanism. Their genetic structure shifted in response to environmental stressors, effectively "learning" how to resist

whatever harmed them.

"We're dealing with an organism unlike anything on Earth," Dr. Samuel muttered to his wife. "It's as if

every part of its biology is designed to counter us.

Whatever hurt them yesterday won't work tomorrow."

Chapter 2

Lillian nodded gravely. "And if this pattern continues, soon there will be nothing left that can harm them."

In the base's common area, the survivors huddled

around a radio, listening as the news unfolded like a grim prophecy. Reports indicated that the

predators had now expanded across the entire

American continent, attacking major cities, towns, and rural communities alike. Each day brought new tales of horror and destruction.

Chapter 2

"This isn't just Cedar Falls anymore," the

announcer's voice crackled over the radio. "From Los Angeles to New York, sightings have been

confirmed. The predators are advancing across the country, adapting and evolving to survive our

counterattacks."

The chilling part was the announcement that the creatures' vulnerability to sunlight was waning. Where once they had lurked in the darkness,

avoiding direct sunlight, they now began venturing out into the daylight hours, their bodies showing no signs of harm from the sun. This shift marked a

terrifying new phase of adaptation.

Hank clenched his fists, feeling a knot of anger and despair in his gut. "They're learning too quickly.

Pretty soon, there won't be any way to stop them."

Dr. Samuel gathered the survivors and laid out the truth, sparing no details. "The predators' evolution is unlike anything we've seen. They're immune to

firearms, immune to sunlight… and soon, they'll be

immune to anything we throw at them. We're

essentially dealing with a super-organism, one that evolves in real time to counter every threat."

Chapter 2

A murmur of panic spread through the group, and one of the civilians, a man named Dan, voiced the fear that everyone was feeling. "So... what are we supposed to do, then? Just wait here and die?"

Emily stood up, her voice steady despite the fear in her eyes. "No. We're not giving up. We're going to

fight back. And my parents might have a plan."

As the days passed, the scientists worked around

the clock, searching for anything that could disrupt the predators' biology. Emily watched as her

parents grew more and more haggard, driven by an obsession to find a solution before it was too late.

One night, Dr. Samuel gathered the survivors in the lab, presenting a radical idea. "We've isolated a

compound from the asteroid fragment," he

explained, holding up a small vial of a glowing,

pale-green liquid. "This compound interacts with the predator's cells in an unusual way. It disrupts

their cellular structure, essentially 'confusing' their adaptation mechanisms."

Chapter 2

Lillian stepped forward, continuing his thought. "If we could administer it, even in small doses, it might slow down their evolution, maybe even make them

vulnerable again. But…" She trailed off, hesitation

clear in her voice.

Hank narrowed his eyes. "But what?"

"We only have enough to make a few doses," Dr.

Samuel replied, his tone grim. "We'd need a direct injection for each predator, and we'd need to hit

their core, where the mutation originates." Emily's

heart sank. "So… we'd have to get up close to them."

"Yes," her father confirmed, looking around the

room. "It's incredibly dangerous, but it's the only

chance we have. This compound might be the key to stopping them— at least for a time."

After much debate, a small team volunteered to administer the compound to a predator. Hank,

Emily, Carl, and a few others trained for the

mission, gathering weapons, protective gear, and the few doses they had. The base's engineers quickly assembled crude harpoon guns, modified to inject the compound directly into a predator's core.

Chapter 2

As they prepared, Emily found herself filled with a mixture of dread and hope. She knew that the odds were stacked against them, but this was their only shot. Hank, ever the optimist, tried to lift the group's spirits.

"Look, we've all faced tough times before," he said with a reassuring grin. "Maybe not this tough, but we're survivors. And if this works, we'll be heroes."

Emily smiled faintly, appreciating his attempt to lighten the mood. They all knew the risks, but they also knew that doing nothing was no longer an option.

The team set out at dawn, moving cautiously through the ruins of Cedar Falls. The predators had taken to hunting during the day, their eyes adapting quickly to withstand sunlight. Emily and the others knew they had to be swift and careful. The plan was to find a single predator, administer the compound, and then return with their observations.

PREDATORS

Chapter 2

They didn't have to search long. In the distance, a lone predator was stalking an abandoned building,

its body glinting in the early light. The creature had mutated further since the last time Emily saw it,

with thicker scales and longer claws, its eyes now a strange blend of pale green and black, like empty

voids.

Hank motioned for silence, raising his hand as he

aimed the modified harpoon gun. They all held their breath as he fired.

The harpoon flew through the air, striking the

creature directly in its side. For a split second, it writhed, its scales trembling as the compound

spread through its system. Emily's heart pounded as she watched, hoping against hope that it would work.

At first, it seemed like the creature was weakening, its movements sluggish and disoriented. But just as a glimmer of hope rose within her, the predator let out a deafening screech, its body convulsing as it

absorbed the compound. In a horrifying instant, it

mutated further, its form shifting and twisting until it stood even larger than before.

Chapter 2

"Run!" Hank shouted, and the team scattered as the predator lunged toward them with renewed fury.

The team ran through the streets, their footsteps echoing in the hollow silence. The predator was

relentless, its every step pounding the ground as it pursued them with terrifying speed. Hank led them through a series of alleys, trying to lose it, but the creature was faster, each second bringing it closer.

Finally, they burst into an abandoned parking

garage, scrambling to hide among the scattered debris. The predator stopped at the entrance,

sniffing the air, its massive form silhouetted

against the daylight. It let out a low, guttural growl as it moved forward, searching.

Emily pressed herself against a concrete pillar, her heart racing. She glanced over at Hank, who

nodded, signaling her to stay still. They held their breath, praying that the creature would lose

interest.

Chapter 2

For a moment, it seemed to work. The predator paused, sniffed the air again, and turned to leave. But then, in a flash, it spun around, charging toward them with a ferocity they had never seen before.

Hank stepped forward, drawing its attention as he fired his last shot. "Emily, go!" he yelled, and the

team scattered, darting out of the parking garage and into the open street. They ran, adrenaline

fueling their every step, as the creature's furious cries faded behind them.

Chapter 2

When they finally returned to the base, exhausted and shaken, the reality of their situation hit them harder than ever. The compound had failed. The

predators were not only resistant—they were thriving.

Dr. Samuel and Lillian listened as the team

recounted their encounter, their faces pale. "If even the compound doesn't work..." Dr. Lillian

whispered, her voice breaking. "Then what are we

supposed to do?"

A heavy silence fell over the room. For the first time, the survivors felt the weight of true

hopelessness. They were outmatched, outgunned, and outsmarted. The predators were no longer just invaders—they were conquerors.

As night fell, Dr. Samuel gathered the group, his

face grim but resolute. "We have one last option. We need to go back to the asteroid itself. If we can find a substance there that they haven't encountered

yet, we might have a chance."

Chapter 2

Emily felt a surge of determination. "I'll go with you. We need to do this... for everyone who's

fallen."

The others agreed, though the decision weighed

heavily on them. They knew the journey would be dangerous, perhaps even fatal. But with the

predators advancing and their last line of defense failing, it was the only hope they had left.

With heavy hearts and steely resolve, the survivors prepared for what would likely be their final

mission: a desperate journey to the heart of the asteroid, where they hoped to find the key to

humanity's survival.

Chapter 3 The Only Hope

The survivors were still reeling from the failure of the compound. The predators were adapting at an alarming rate, their mutations seemingly endless.

Even in daylight, their once-blind yellowish eyes glinted with a terrifying clarity, the predators

having quickly developed partial immunity to

sunlight. It felt as though the creatures were two steps ahead, constantly evolving faster than

humanity could respond.

Emily sat in the corner of the lab, exhausted and weighed down with grief. The team had scattered

in the escape, and Hank—fearless, brave Hank—had vanished during the chase. No one had seen him

fall, but the silence about his fate cast a heavy shadow over them all.

"We lost Hank," she whispered, voice cracking.

Chapter 3

Carl placed a reassuring hand on her shoulder, but she could see the same sorrow in his eyes. Losing Hank felt like losing their last bit of hope.

Days passed with no word or sight of Hank. Dr.

Samuel and Lillian threw themselves into more

desperate research, but Emily and the rest of the

team were restless. They needed to fight back, and they needed to know if anything could kill these

creatures.

Then, one night, a small group ventured out into the open once again. Armed with what little they

had left, they had one goal: to find another predator and observe its behavior up close, despite the

danger.

As they crept through the outskirts of town, a

familiar low growl stopped them in their tracks.

Emerging from the darkness, a predator appeared,

its yellowish eyes reflecting the moonlight. Emily's heart pounded as it moved toward them, its form

even more monstrous than before. Its thick scales

glistened, its mouth hanging slightly open to reveal rows of jagged teeth.

Chapter 3

Carl, aimed his gun and fired, hitting the predator

squarely in the chest. The creature staggered, but it quickly steadied itself, unfazed by the attack. Emily gritted her teeth. This was futile; bullets barely

scratched the surface of these beasts anymore.

Carl emptied all o his bullets becoming frustrated and then threw a pointed stick into the predator' s heart. It penetrated in.

"What the ...," he hissed to the others. "How can it be?"

Emily's eyes widened. "I think that they are still not adapted to natural things because we ar not using

them to kill it."

" That would be correct.", Carl sighed.

As they returned to base with the new discovery, the radio crackled to life with an urgent message. Static filled the air, followed by a voice that made everyone freeze in their tracks.

Chapter 3

"This is Hank. I... I'm alive. Don't know if you all can hear me, but I'm at the outskirts, by the old

water tower. I found a way. I killed that predator. I had hit him in the mouth, right where their teeth

end and the flesh begins. That's their weakness. I've... I've taken down a few of them this way."

Emily's heart skipped a beat, and a wave of relief washed over her. She glanced at Carl, a smile

breaking through the exhaustion on her face.

"He's alive," she whispered, almost afraid to believe it. "Hank is alive!"

Ignoring the pleas to wait, Emily and Carl sprinted out of the base, armed and desperate to find their friend. The town was eerily quiet as they moved

through the darkened streets, their footsteps

echoing against the empty buildings. Then, by the old water tower, they spotted a figure moving

toward them.

It was Hank, battered and bruised, but very much

alive. In his hands, he held his trusty shotgun, now smeared with dark green blood—the blood of the

predators.

Chapter 3

"Hank!" Emily shouted, running to him and throwing her arms around him. He chuckled, wincing slightly at the embrace.

"Hey, I'm not that easy to get rid of," he said, his

voice a blend of exhaustion and humor. "I managed to take down a few of them on my own. Those

things are relentless, but they can be stopped if you know where to hit."

Carl clapped him on the back, grinning. "You're a damn legend, Hank. You found their weakness

before any of us did."

Hank nodded, a glint of satisfaction in his eyes. "I

figured it out by accident. They attacked in a group, and when I fired into one's mouth, it went down.

Almost like its whole system shuts down when you hit the right spot."

Back at the base, Hank shared every detail of his

experience with the predators. He explained how he had discovered their vulnerability by observing

their behavior, their strength, and how they always hesitated before attacking with their mouths open.

Chapter 3

Dr. Samuel, inspired by Hank's discovery,

developed a more strategic plan for the team. He gathered everyone in the main hall, a makeshift map of Cedar Falls spread out before them.

"Here's what we're going to do," he began. "We'll lure the predators out one by one, using their

attraction to movement and sound. When they come in close, we target the inside of their mouths, right at the core. It's dangerous, yes, but with Hank's

discovery, we stand a real chance."

A murmur of agreement rippled through the group, a faint spark of hope lighting their tired faces. They had a plan, a method to fight back—and they had

Hank to thank for it.

As they prepared their weapons and finalized their strategy, Hank and Emily shared a quiet moment.

Despite the grimness surrounding them, there was an unspoken bond between them—a mutual respect forged in the fires of survival.

Chapter 3

"Thanks, Hank," Emily said softly. "For not giving up."

He shrugged, a hint of a smile playing at his lips. "Wouldn't dream of it. Besides, we're in this

together, all of us."

That night, the team put their new plan into action.

Moving stealthily through the town, they set up makeshift traps—cans filled with rocks, old car

alarms rigged to sound on a timer, anything that would attract the predators' attention.

It didn't take long for the creatures to show. The first predator appeared in the distance, its

yellowish eyes scanning the area, honing in on the noise. Its massive form loomed in the darkness, a terrifying sight that sent chills down everyone's

spine.

Hank was the first to fire, timing his shot perfectly as the creature opened its mouth to snarl. His bullet hit the mark, and the predator fell to the ground

with a furious shriek, convulsing as its life ebbed away.

Chapter 3

Emily and Carl followed suit, each of them taking down a predator with calculated precision. Their

nerves were stretched to the breaking point, but the plan was working. One by one, the creatures fell,

their weakness exploited to deadly effect.

By dawn, the team had managed to thin the

predators' numbers significantly. They returned to base, exhausted but triumphant, the weight of hope a tangible force among them. For the first time

since the asteroid fell, they felt as though they were gaining the upper hand.

Dr. Samuel, watching the survivors return with

weary but victorious smiles, couldn't help but feel a glimmer of optimism. Perhaps, with enough time,

they could turn the tide. Perhaps this was the beginning of humanity's resurgence.

But as the group settled in to rest, a familiar growl echoed from the shadows. Emerging from the edge of the base was a new predator—larger, faster, and with an intensity in its yellow eyes that chilled

them all to the bone.

It had been watching them. Observing.

Chapter 3

The new predator lunged forward, its movements quicker and more calculated than the others. Emily and Hank barely had time to react, dodging as it tore through the air where they'd been standing moments before. Its yellow eyes seemed to focus directly on them, following their every movement with an intelligence they hadn't seen before.

"Everyone, fall back!" Dr. Lillian shouted, her voice edged with terror. "It's learning! It knows!"

They retreated, scrambling back into the safety of the base as the creature prowled outside, studying them with a terrifying patience.

Hank took a steadying breath, his grip tightening on his weapon. "We might've taught it something," he murmured. "It knows our tactics now."

Emily's heart sank. The creatures were evolving once more, adapting to even their newfound strategy. It was as if the predators could read their minds, absorbing every trick, every technique they used against them.

Chapter 3

As they fortified the base and prepared for the next onslaught, Dr. Samuel pulled Emily aside, his

expression grave.

"There's only one place left where we might find a way to stop this," he said. "The asteroid. If there's any chance of finding something there that could end this for good, we have to take it."

Emily nodded, determination hardening her gaze. "Then we go," she replied. "We'll do whatever it

takes."

As the team braced themselves for their final mission, they knew that the path ahead was bleak. The predators were relentless, adaptive, and terrifyingly intelligent. But they had a spark of hope, however small—and that was enough to keep them moving forward.

The atmosphere in the bunker was tense as the

survivors processed the latest attack. Everyone was on edge, but hope flickered faintly in the air. In the lab, Hank, Emily, Dr. Samuel, and Dr. Lillian

huddled around a microscope, the bright light illuminating their faces in the dim room.

Chapter 3

"Look at this," Dr. Lillian said, her voice trembling with excitement as she adjusted the lens. "This is

from the samples Emily collected after the last

encounter. We've been analyzing it for days, and there's something here—something we didn't see before."

Emily leaned in, squinting at the screen as Dr. Lillian focused on a peculiar compound that shimmered under the microscope. "What are we looking at?"

"It appears to be a biochemical reaction," Dr.

Samuel replied, pointing at a cluster of cells that

were rapidly multiplying. "These compounds have a unique structure that reacts aggressively to the

predator's biological makeup. It could be the key to neutralizing them."

Hank's heart raced as he processed the

implications. "You mean to say we can create something—something that can actually harm them?"

Chapter 3

"Yes," Dr. Lillian said, her eyes gleaming with hope. "If we can isolate and synthesize this compound, we might have a weapon against them."

With renewed purpose, the team dedicated

themselves to isolating the compound. They worked tirelessly, day and night, the bunker filled with the sounds of beeping machines, scribbling notes, and

hurried discussions. As the sun rose and set outside, time lost all meaning.

Emily became the main point of contact for the

samples. She had learned how to handle the alien organisms with care, ensuring that the precious

material was preserved. Each sample they examined revealed more about the predators' biology, their

vulnerabilities, and how they adapted so rapidly.

"Look here," Hank pointed to a series of graphs that mapped the predators' evolutionary traits. "If we

understand this pattern, we can predict their next moves. It's like a playbook for their adaptations."

Chapter 3

"That's brilliant!" Emily exclaimed, her exhaustion momentarily forgotten. "If we can forecast their

changes, we can prepare better defenses."

As they dove deeper into the research, it became clear that they were on the brink of a significant breakthrough. Each day brought new revelations

about the alien species they had come to dread, and yet, their findings offered a glimmer of hope.

Finally, after nearly a week of relentless work, Dr. Lillian announced that they were ready to conduct their first experiment with the new compound. The

atmosphere in the lab was electric with anticipation and anxiety.

"We'll need a live specimen," she explained, her voice steady despite the tension. "We have to be

careful. If we can get our hands on one, we can test the compound's effects."

Chapter 3

The group exchanged glances, understanding the gravity of the situation. They had to go back

outside, back into the heart of the danger, and it wouldn't be easy.

"We can set a trap," Hank suggested, his

determination evident. "We know how to lure them now. We can attract one to a secluded area,

administer the compound, and see what happens

Emily nodded, her heart pounding. "Let's do it. We have to know if this works

As they formulated their plan, the mood shifted.

They were no longer just survivors; they were fighters, ready to take back control from the predators that had upended their lives."

The following night, the team ventured into the

outskirts of Cedar Falls, armed with weapons and

vials of the newly synthesized compound. The moon hung low in the sky, casting an eerie glow over the desolate landscape.

Chapter 3

Hank, Emily, and Carl carefully placed makeshift traps baited with sounds—old radios tuned to static and motion sensors rigged to alert them when a predator approached. They positioned themselves strategically, hiding behind the remnants of abandoned cars and debris.

"Remember," Hank instructed quietly. "We need to wait until it's close, then strike when it opens its mouth. That's when we'll inject the compound."

Hours passed, tension thickening in the air. Every rustle of leaves or distant howl sent their hearts racing. Then, finally, they heard it—a deep, guttural growl echoing through the night.

The predator emerged from the shadows, its yellowish eyes glinting with hunger. It prowled closer, nostrils flaring as it caught the scent of their bait.

"Now!" Hank whispered urgently.

Chapter 3

As the predator neared, Hank and Carl stepped out from their hiding spots, weapons raised. Emily held the syringe filled with the compound, her hands

steady despite the adrenaline coursing through her veins. The predator hesitated, its eyes darting

around, sensing danger.

"Draw it in!" Hank shouted.

Carl threw a rock to the side, distracting the

creature. As it turned, its mouth opened, and in that split second, Emily lunged forward, plunging the

syringe into its throat. The predator roared,

thrashing in pain as the compound coursed through its system.

The reaction was instantaneous and terrifying. The predator convulsed, muscles spasming violently. It fell to the ground, shrieking, as its body reacted to the compound with a force they had not

anticipated.

"It's working!" Emily shouted, exhilaration flooding her senses. "Look at it!"

Chapter 3

The creature writhed, its body twisting unnaturally, the yellowish glow in its eyes flickering as it

struggled against the effects of the compound. The team watched in awe as the creature's form began to shift, its scales bubbling and rippling.

But their triumph was short-lived. The predator

suddenly let out a piercing howl, a sound so full of

rage and pain that it sent shivers down their spines. It clawed at the ground, trying to escape the effects of the compound, but it was losing the battle.

"Back up! It's going to explode!" Carl yelled, and they all scrambled away as the predator's body began to swell.

In a terrifying flash, the creature erupted, a shower of scales and viscera spraying the area around

them. Emily fell back, barely avoiding the gruesome shower, her heart racing from the chaos of the

moment.

When the dust settled, the team regrouped, their hearts pounding .

Chapter 3

They had managed to take down a predator, and it was a significant victory. But the atmosphere was heavy with the weight of what they had witnessed.

"We did it," Hank said breathlessly. "We actually did it."

Dr. Lillian knelt beside the remnants of the

predator, examining the ground. "We need to

analyze what just happened," she said. "This might give us insight into the compound's effectiveness

and how we can improve it."

As they gathered samples of the predator's remains,

Emily's thoughts drifted. They had successfully

neutralized one predator, but how many more were out there? And could the compound work against

the others?

Back at the bunker, they immediately began

analyzing the samples. Emily and Dr. Lillian worked side by side, studying the genetic makeup of the

predator and the effects of the compound. As the hours turned into days, they made astonishing

progress.

Chapter 3

"Look at this," Dr. Lillian said one evening, pointing at a series of charts on the screen. "The compound

seems to affect the neurological pathways of the predator. It disrupts their ability to process

information and coordinate their movements."

Emily leaned closer, a grin breaking across her face. "That means we can create a stronger version, one

that can incapacitate them more effectively."

"Exactly," Dr. Lillian said, her excitement palpable. "If we refine this compound, we might be able to

create a weapon strong enough to take down a whole group."

The team worked feverishly, each breakthrough building on the last. They refined the compound, adjusting its chemical structure to enhance its

lethality against the predators. Days turned into a blur of scientific discovery and experimentation, and with each success, the atmosphere in the

bunker grew more hopeful.

Chapter 3

With the compound nearing its final form, Dr.

Samuel called the team together once more. "We need a new plan," he stated firmly. "We've

successfully taken down one predator, but we need to understand how to deploy this compound

effectively in a larger scale."

Hank nodded, "If we can lure them into a confined space, we could potentially take down an entire

group."

"I suggest we set up a trap in the heart of the city," Emily proposed. "We can use the old town square.

It's wide open and we can create a distraction to draw them in."

Dr. Samuel considered the idea. "That could work,

but it's risky. We need to be sure we have a way out in case it goes wrong."

"Let's set up a perimeter," Hank said, determination shining in his eyes. "We can fortify the area and

have escape routes planned. If we do this right, we could cripple the predator population in one go."

Chapter 3

The team spent the next few days preparing, gathering supplies and laying out the trap. Emily felt a renewed sense of purpose as they worked together, driven by the shared goal of saving their community.

The night before the operation, the bunker was filled with a nervous energy. Everyone knew that they were on the brink of something significant, but uncertainty lingered in the air.

Emily found herself in the lab late that night, staring at the vials of the compound lined up neatly on the table. Each one held the promise of hope, but also the weight of responsibility. She couldn't shake the thought of the lives they were risking, including her own.

Hank entered the lab, sensing her unease. "Hey," he said softly, stepping beside her. "You okay?"

"Just thinking," Emily replied, her voice barely above a whisper. "What if we fail? What if we don't make it back?"

Chapter 3

Hank placed a reassuring hand on her shoulder. "We can't think like that. We have a plan, and we're

ready. We're going to make a difference."

She smiled, grateful for his unwavering support. "I just wish we had more time."

"Time is a luxury we don't have," he said, looking out at the darkness beyond the bunker walls. "But we're going to give it our best shot."

They stood in silence for a moment, both aware of the impending battle and the uncertainty it

brought. But as they prepared to face the predators once more, a shared resolve ignited within them.

The next morning, they set out for the town square, the weight of their mission heavy on their

shoulders. Each step felt like a march toward the unknown, the air thick with tension.

They arrived at the square, and the sight was surreal. Buildings loomed over them, shadows

stretching across the pavement. Emily's heart raced as she scanned the area, her instincts heightened.

Chapter 3

"Let's get everything set up," Hank instructed, the urgency in his voice propelling them into action.

As they worked, the reality of their situation began to settle in. They were luring the predators into a

trap, risking everything for a chance at surviva

With each passing moment, the town square

transformed into a battleground. The traps were set, the compound ready for deployment. They

stood together, waiting for the inevitable clash that would determine their fate.

As dusk fell, the first sounds of predators echoed through the streets. The team huddled behind

cover, adrenaline surging as they prepared for the oncoming threat.

"Here they come!" Carl shouted, pointing toward the shadows that slithered between the buildings.

Emily gripped her weapon tightly, heart racing. The predators emerged, eyes gleaming in the dim light, and a chill ran down her spine. The hunters were

now the hunted.

Chapter 3

"Now!" Hank yelled, and the team activated the traps.

Chaos erupted as the predators charged into the square. The team unleashed the compound,

targeting the creatures with precision. The air filled with the sound of snarls and screams as the

compound took effect, wreaking havoc on the predators.

Emily watched in awe as the creatures thrashed and twisted, their bodies succumbing to the effects of

the compound. They were gaining ground, but the predators were adapting quickly, learning from

their mistakes.

"Keep pushing!" Dr. Lillian shouted, urging them forward. "We can't let up now!"

As the battle raged on, the predators started to fight back with ferocity. One of the creatures

lunged toward Hank, its jaws snapping inches from his face.

Chapter 3

"Watch out!" Emily cried, rushing to his side.

In a split-second decision, she thrust her weapon

forward, firing a round into the creature's throat. It stumbled, and Hank took advantage, delivering a

lethal blow to its midsection.

But there were more, so many more. The predators were relentless, and Emily's heart sank as she

realized the odds were stacked against them. They were outnumbered and losing ground.

Just then, a loud explosion echoed through the square, shaking the ground beneath them. The

distraction caught the attention of the predators, and in that moment of chaos, Emily seized the

opportunity.

"Fall back!" she shouted, leading the team toward

their escape route. They moved swiftly, adrenaline fueling their every action.

Chapter 3

As they navigated the maze of buildings, the predators pursued them, their yellowish eyes

gleaming in the dark. Emily's pulse raced as she glanced back, fear gripping her heart.

"We need to regroup!" Hank yelled, urgency in his voice.

They ducked into an alley, panting heavily as they paused to catch their breath. The sounds of the

predators echoed in the distance, a chilling reminder of the danger they faced.

"We can't keep this up," Dr. Samuel gasped, leaning against the wall. "We need a new plan."

Emily felt a wave of desperation wash over her.

"What if we create a diversion? Something to draw them away while we regroup and plan our next

move."

Hank nodded, his mind racing. "If we can find

something that creates a loud noise, we could lure them in another direction."

Chapter 3

"I saw some old machinery at the factory down the street," Carl suggested. "If we can rig it to create a loud sound, it might work."

"Let's go," Emily urged, determination fueling her resolve. They couldn't give up now—not when they were so close.

They raced toward the factory, the weight of the

moment heavy on their shoulders. The atmosphere was thick with tension as they approached, knowing they had one last chance to turn the tide.

Inside the factory, they quickly scavenged for supplies, gathering anything that could create noise. They rigged machinery to create a loud, deafening sound, hoping to draw the predators away.

"Once it's ready, we'll need to make a run for it,"

Hank said, urgency in his voice. "We need to act fast before they catch up." With the machinery set, they hurried outside, the noise echoing through the

night. As they watched the predators shift

direction, a surge of hope filled Emily's heart.

Chapter 3

"Now!" Hank shouted, and they sprinted toward the makeshift barricade they had set up earlier.

As they reached the barricade, the sound of the

machinery reached a crescendo, drowning out the noise of the predators. They scrambled behind the barricade, catching their breath as they prepared for the final push.

But the predators were smart. Even distracted, they could sense the team's presence, their instincts

honed by evolution. A few of the creatures began to circle back, realizing the trap.

"Get ready!" Hank yelled as he raised his weapon, adrenaline coursing through his veins.

Emily felt the weight of fear and determination collide within her. This was their last stand, the

moment that could determine the fate of humanity against these relentless predators.

Chapter 3

The first predator lunged at them, its jaws snapping dangerously close. Emily fired, hitting the creature in the shoulder, but it only staggered for a moment before retaliating. The team fought with everything they had, firing their weapons and using the

compound at every opportunity.

"Push them back!" Dr. Samuel shouted, desperately trying to keep the predators at bay.

As they fought, Emily's heart raced. She felt the adrenaline surge through her, every instinct

screaming at her to survive. But just as they began to regain control, more predators emerged from the shadows, their numbers overwhelming.

"We need to retreat!" Carl shouted, panic in his voice.

"No!" Hank yelled, determination burning in his eyes. "We can't let them take us down now!"

As the battle raged on, the team fought valiantly, but the tide was turning. The predators adapted quickly, their yellowish eyes glimmering with a

chilling intelligence.

Chapter 3

With each passing moment, the predators grew

bolder, attacking with ferocity. Emily felt the fear

clawing at her heart, but she couldn't afford to give in. They were on the brink of something significant; they had to push through.

Suddenly, a loud roar echoed through the square,

and a massive predator emerged from the darkness, larger than any they had encountered before. Its

yellow eyes burned with rage, and Emily's heart sank.

"We can't fight that thing!" she shouted, panic rising within her.

Hank's expression hardened. "We have to try!"

As the colossal predator lunged at them, the team scrambled to evade its attack. The ground shook beneath them as it crashed into their barricade,

sending debris flying.

"Fall back!" Dr. Lillian cried, but it was too late. The predator was upon them, and chaos erupted.

Chapter 3

In the chaos, the team fought valiantly, but the massive predator was relentless. One by one, they fell back, struggling to regroup as the creature tore through their defenses.

Emily felt despair creeping in as she realized how outmatched they were. They had come so far, but it felt like it was all slipping away.

"Keep fighting!" Hank shouted, his voice full of determination. "We can't let them win!"

With renewed resolve, they pushed back, using every ounce of strength they had left. Emily fired her weapon at the massive predator, but it was like throwing pebbles at a wall.

Just when it seemed all hope was lost, the compound they had synthesized ignited a spark within her. "The compound!" she shouted, suddenly realizing their last chance.

"Everyone! We need to combine the compound with our remaining ammunition!" Emily urged, scrambling to load the ammunition with the compound's remnants.

Chapter 3

In a moment of sheer desperation, they worked

together, loading bullets with the potent compound as the massive predator lunged again.

With the new ammunition ready, the team steadied their weapons, hearts pounding as the colossal

predator charged them once more.

"Now!" Hank shouted, and they unleashed a barrage of gunfire, each bullet packed with the compound's lethal potential. The predator staggered, howling in agony as the compound took effect. It fell to the

ground, its massive body thrashing violently before going still.

As the dust settled, the team looked at each other in disbelief. They had managed to take down the

largest predator yet, a significant victory in the battle against the alien threat.

But as they caught their breath, reality hit hard.

The night had taken its toll, and the cost of their victory was steep. They had lost friends and allies in the fight, their numbers dwindling as the

predators continued to adapt and evolve.

Chapter 3

"We need to regroup and reassess," Dr. Samuel said, his voice heavy with the weight of their losses.

"This isn't over. We need to learn from this."

Emily nodded, her heart aching for those they had lost. "We have to keep fighting. We owe it to them."

As they made their way back to the bunker, the sun began to rise, illuminating the devastation left in

the wake of their battle. But amidst the destruction, a flicker of hope remained— the knowledge that they had the power to fight back, to protect what

remained of their world.

Back at the bunker, the atmosphere was heavy with grief but also determination. They knew the fight

was far from over. The predators were still out

there, evolving faster than they could anticipate.

Emily and the team gathered to assess their next

steps, each of them acutely aware of the urgency of their mission.

"We need to analyze the data from the last

encounter," Dr. Lillian suggested. "Every detail could be crucial for our next plan of attack."

Chapter 3

Hank nodded, his expression serious. "We need to understand how they're adapting. We can't afford to be caught off guard again."

As they reviewed their findings, Emily felt a renewed sense of purpose. They were on the brink of discovering something significant, and she was determined to see it through.

Days turned into weeks as they worked tirelessly in the bunker, analyzing data and refining their tactics. Each day brought new challenges, but also new breakthroughs.

Their findings on the compound allowed them to enhance its effectiveness, and they developed new strategies to combat the predators' evolving nature.

The atmosphere was charged with hope as they prepared for the next phase of their fight.

But as they strategized, a lingering question remained: how long could they hold out against the predators? Each day felt like a ticking clock, a countdown to the inevitable confrontation that lay ahead.

Chapter 3

Emily looked around the bunker at her fellow

survivors, each one carrying the weight of loss and determination. They were in this together, bound

by a shared purpose to reclaim their world from the clutches of the predators.

As they prepared for the next battle, a flicker of hope ignited within her. They might be fighting against insurmountable odds, but they were not alone. Together, they would rise against the

darkness and face whatever came their way.

Chapter 4 The King

In the days following their last encounter with the predators, the mood in the bunker shifted from

determination to desperation. Though they had

experienced small victories, the relentless advance of the predators weighed heavily on every

survivor's mind. Every night brought new reports of attacks, of entire towns falling silent as the

predators hunted.

The scientists worked tirelessly, pouring over data and analyzing the remnants of the predators they had collected. It was during one of these late-night sessions that Dr. Lillian made a shocking

discovery.

"Everyone, listen up!" she called, gathering the team in the main lab. Her voice was laced with

urgency, pulling Emily and Hank from their tasks.

Chapter 4

"What is it?" Hank asked, concern etched across his face.

"I think I've found a way to end this," Dr. Lillian said, her eyes wide with a mixture of excitement

and fear. "The asteroid that brought the initial wave of predators—there's something about it, something we haven't fully explored. If we can analyze its

core, we might be able to harness a compound that can kill them all at once."

Emily's heart raced at the possibility. "You mean the asteroid itself could hold the key to defeating the predators?"

"Exactly," Dr. Lillian confirmed. "But we'll need a sample from the main body of the asteroid to

confirm my theory. This could be our only chance."

"Is it still safe to approach?" Carl asked, glancing at the monitors that showed satellite images of the

area.

"We have no choice," Dr. Samuel replied. "We're running out of time. The predators are evolving

faster than we can react. We need to take the risk."

Chapter 4

As the team deliberated the plan, Hank stood with his arms crossed, the weight of their situation

heavy on his shoulders. "Let's do it. If we can find a way to use the asteroid against them, we owe it to

everyone we've lost."

The following day, they gathered their gear and prepared for the journey to the impact site. A

convoy of modified vehicles—armor-plated and heavily armed—was loaded with weapons, the

precious Anti-Predator Compound, and the

scientific equipment needed for their research.

Emily's heart pounded in her chest, the anticipation mingling with dread as they set out.

The landscape had changed dramatically since the initial impact. What once was a bustling town was now a ghostly wasteland, buildings crumbling and

streets littered with debris. The sky hung low, thick with clouds that seemed to mirror the gloom in

their hearts.

Chapter 4

As they approached the impact zone, the atmosphere shifted. An eerie silence enveloped the convoy, the only sound being the crunch of tires on gravel. Emily peered out of the window, her gaze fixed on the horizon where the asteroid had crashed. The site was now surrounded by a thick, unnatural fog that swirled ominously.

"We need to stay alert," Hank cautioned, scanning the area. "If the predators have taken control of this area, we could be walking into a trap."

"Let's stick together," Dr. Lillian instructed, her voice steady despite the tension. "We can't afford to lose anyone else."

As they disembarked, the heavy silence settled around them, broken only by the rustling of leaves and the distant sounds of nature. The asteroid lay ahead, a jagged mass protruding from the earth, but as they approached, something felt off.

Chapter 4

As they neared the asteroid, the ground began to

tremble beneath their feet. Emily's pulse quickened as she exchanged worried glances with the others.

Suddenly, the fog thickened, swirling violently

around them, and a guttural roar echoed through the air.

"What was that?" Carl shouted, raising his weapon.

Before anyone could respond, a massive creature lunged from the fog. It was unlike any predator

they had encountered before—taller and more

muscular, with sleek, obsidian skin that shimmered in the dim light. But what struck them most was its eyes—brilliant blue, burning with an intelligence

that sent chills down Emily's spine.

"The King Predator," Dr. Samuel breathed, eyes wide with horror. "It's the apex of their evolution."

As the creature advanced, the air crackled with a palpable energy, a fierce aura surrounding it. This was no ordinary predator; it was a guardian, a

protector of the asteroid, and it exuded power beyond their understanding.

Chapter 4

"Fall back!" Hank ordered, backing away slowly. "We need to regroup!"

But the King Predator wasn't interested in retreat.

It let out another bone-chilling roar, charging

forward with terrifying speed. Emily barely had time to react as it lunged toward them, massive jaws snapping inches from her face.

Chapter 4

In the chaos, the team scrambled to defend

themselves. Hank fired his weapon, but the bullets seemed to bounce harmlessly off the King

Predator's armored skin. It was as if they were nothing more than an annoyance.

"Use the Anti-Predator Compound!" Dr. Lillian yelled, desperation in her voice.

The team quickly regrouped, combining their

efforts to deploy the compound. They unleashed a

volley of the specially designed ammunition, but as the compound struck the King Predator, it barely

flinched.

"What's happening? It should be working!" Emily shouted, panic rising within her.

"It's too evolved," Dr. Samuel gasped, fear etched on his face. "The compound isn't effective against it!"

The realization hit Emily like a punch to the gut. The King Predator was unlike any enemy they had faced; it had adapted to withstand their most

powerful weapon.

Chapter 4

"Retreat!" Hank shouted, waving them back. "We can't fight it like this!"

But the King Predator had other plans. With a

powerful swipe of its massive claws, it sent Carl

crashing against the asteroid, his screams echoing through the air. The team froze, horror-stricken.

"No! Carl!" Dr. Lillian cried, rushing forward, but Emily grabbed her arm, holding her back.

"It's too dangerous!" Emily shouted. "We have to get out of here!"

With the King Predator focused on them, the team began their frantic retreat. They dodged debris and scrambled over fallen rocks, desperately trying to distance themselves from the monstrous creature.

Emily's heart raced as she glanced back, fear gripping her throat as she watched the King Predator pursue them.

Chapter 4

The sound of its growls reverberated through the air, a chilling reminder of the terror that hunted them. They rushed back toward the vehicles, but the path was fraught with danger. The King

Predator was gaining on them, its speed unmatched.

"Get to the vehicles!" Hank shouted, urging everyone forward. "Now!"

They sprinted as fast as they could, adrenaline

fueling their movements. Emily's lungs burned as she pushed herself to keep up with the others, but the King Predator was relentless, its blue eyes

locked onto its prey.

As they reached the vehicles, Dr. Lillian fumbled
with the door, her hands shaking with fear. "Hurry! Get in!"

Just as they clambered inside, the ground shook

violently, and the King Predator lunged, its massive form crashing against the side of the vehicle. The

impact sent them sprawling, and Emily's heart

raced as she realized how close they were to being caught.

Chapter 4

"Go! Go!" Hank shouted, slamming his foot on the gas pedal as the vehicle lurched forward, narrowly

escaping the King Predator's grasp. They sped away from the impact site, the creature's furious roars

fading into the distance.

As they drove, Emily felt the adrenaline coursing through her veins, a mix of relief and lingering

terror. They had escaped, but the encounter had left them shaken.

"What the hell was that?" Carl gasped, clutching his side where he had hit the asteroid.

"The King Predator," Dr. Lillian said, her voice

trembling. "It's the apex of their evolution, and it's protecting the asteroid."

"We need to regroup and figure out a new plan,"

Hank said, determination returning to his voice. "If the asteroid holds the key to defeating the

predators, we can't give up now."

Chapter 4

Emily nodded, her mind racing. They had faced the King Predator and survived, but the knowledge that it was out there, evolving and growing stronger,

weighed heavily on her heart.

Back at the bunker, the atmosphere was thick with tension. The team gathered around the table,

replaying the encounter in their minds. They were alive, but the encounter had exposed the terrifying reality of their situation.

"The King Predator is not just a creature; it's a

sentinel," Dr. Samuel said, his voice steady. "It's protecting the asteroid, and we need to figure out why."

Emily looked around the room, meeting the gazes of her fellow survivors. They were all grappling with

the knowledge that they had barely escaped with their lives, but they also had a new mission—a

chance to end the reign of the predators.

"We need to study the asteroid," she said, her voice firm. "If there's something in it that can help us, we need to find it. We can't let the King Predator stop us."

Chapter 4

As they strategized, the team quickly realized that they would need a different approach. They had to gather more intel on the King Predator and the

asteroid's core. It was clear that they needed to study its behavior, learn how it operated, and

understand what made it tick.

"We could set up a surveillance system," Dr. Lillian suggested. "If we can monitor the area around the asteroid, we might be able to gather information

without putting ourselves in danger."

Hank nodded. "We'll need to work in shifts, keeping a constant watch on the asteroid and the King

Predator's movements. We can't let our guard down."

With a renewed sense of purpose, the team began to prepare for the next phase of their plan. They

gathered equipment, set up cameras, and made

contingency plans for their surveillance operation.

Chapter 4

Days turned into a blur of activity as they monitored the area around the asteroid, piecing together the behaviors of the King Predator. The tension hung heavy in the air, but as they observed its movements, a flicker of hope ignited within them.

"We're learning," Emily said one evening as they reviewed the footage. "The King Predator has a pattern. It seems to retreat to a specific area at certain times. We might be able to exploit that."

"We can't act recklessly," Hank reminded her, but his eyes shone with determination. "If we can catch it off guard, we might have a chance."

As they continued their surveillance, Emily felt a growing sense of urgency. They were racing against time, and the stakes were higher than ever. The predators were still advancing, and the world beyond the bunker was crumbling.

But amid the darkness, they had a glimmer of hope.

They were learning, adapting, and preparing for their next confrontation with the King Predator.

Chapter 4

As the days passed, a strange calm settled over the bunker. They were growing more confident in their understanding of the King Predator, but the tension was still palpable. Each member of the team

understood that the next encounter could tip the balance between survival and annihilation.

One night, as they gathered around the table for a

late-night strategy session, Emily felt the weight of their situation pressing down on her. They had lost so much already, and she was acutely aware of the

fragility of their hope.

"I know we're all tired," she said, glancing around the table at the weary faces of her friends and

allies. "But we can't afford to let our guard down.

We need to stay focused and be ready for anything."

Hank nodded, his expression serious. "We've come too far to turn back now. We owe it to those we've lost to see this through."

Chapter 4

As they prepared for the final confrontation with the King Predator, Emily's heart raced with a

mixture of fear and determination. They had one

chance to reclaim their world, and she was ready to fight for it.

Chapter 5 The Final Stand

Amidst the chaos at the asteroid site, Carl had acted on pure instinct. When the King Predator lunged toward Hank and the others, his heart

pounded as he realized it was his chance. Darting behind the cover of shattered rocks, he slipped

closer to the asteroid's exposed surface, barely

keeping his balance as he approached. The glinting, jagged surface held a dark, almost hypnotic allure, a reminder of the unknown forces that had brought the predators to Earth.

With careful precision, Carl unsealed a small

containment vial and chipped away a piece of the asteroid. The rock seemed to pulse with an eerie energy, faint tendrils of heat rising from its core.

He stowed the sample and retreated just as the

earth beneath him trembled from the force of the King Predator's roars.

Chapter 5

As he looked over his shoulder, he saw Hank and the others desperately trying to evade the King

Predator's massive claws. The creature's blue eyes blazed with fury, its jaws snapping as it pursued

them through the rubble. Carl swallowed hard, guilt and fear twisting his stomach. He knew there was

no way to save them without endangering the mission—and perhaps the survival of humanity.

When Carl finally rejoined the team at their

rendezvous point, his hands were shaking. He held up the containment vial with the asteroid sample, his voice barely a whisper. "I got it. We have what we need to make the weapon."

The team, battered and breathless, looked at him with a mixture of relief and disbelief. Emily's gaze softened, her voice steady but laced with concern. "You... you did it?"

Carl nodded, glancing down at the ground. "The

King was focused on you all, and I saw my chance. I'm sorry I left you back there, but we needed this sample."

Chapter 5

Hank clapped a hand on Carl's shoulder, his face still bruised and dirty from the encounter. "Don't

apologize. You did what needed to be done. Without that sample, we don't stand a chance."

Carl's relief was palpable, but he could see the shadows in everyone's eyes. They had narrowly

escaped with their lives, but the true battle was still ahead. He knew they would have to risk

everything if they were going to take down the King Predator and reclaim their world.

Back at the bunker, the team immediately set to work. Dr. Lillian and Dr. Samuel analyzed the

sample Carl had gathered, their faces etched with a new intensity. The compound they'd previously

developed—now dubbed the "Anti-Predator

Compound"—had been close but insufficient. This asteroid sample was the missing link.

Chapter 5

Back in the bunker, as they studied the samples and analyzed the data gathered from their encounter

with the King Predator, Dr. Lillian made a startling discovery. She paced, her eyes glued to the monitor, her mind racing. The asteroid emitted a unique

electromagnetic frequency that matched the

predators' brainwave patterns. It was as if the asteroid were their hive mind, the core of their existence.

"Everyone," Dr. Lillian said, her voice tense with urgency. "The predators are all connected. Every

single one of them is linked to the asteroid's energy field. If we could disrupt that field, we might be

able to sever their connection and kill them all."

Emily's eyes widened, her pulse quickening. "You're saying if we could disable the asteroid, we might be able to wipe them out—completely?"

"Yes," Dr. Lillian replied, her face pale but resolute. "But we'd need to inject a concentrated form of the Anti-Predator Compound directly into the

asteroid's core. That's the only way we could cause a system-wide shutdown of their network."

Chapter 5

A sense of hope surged through the group, quickly tempered by the realization of the dangers

involved. They would have to return to the asteroid site, face the King Predator once again, and deliver the compound to the heart of the asteroid.

Emily, Hank, Carl, and the remaining team members gathered their gear, steeling themselves for what

they all understood would likely be their last

mission. As they loaded up, each member took a

moment to say silent goodbyes—to each other and to the lives they'd left behind.

In the early dawn, they made their way back to the asteroid, moving swiftly and silently, adrenaline

and dread mingling in their veins. The King

Predator's lair loomed ahead, its massive form

casting long, ominous shadows over the twisted landscape.

"Stick to the plan," Hank murmured, glancing at each of them in turn. "We get in, plant the

compound, and get out. No heroics."

Chapter 5

The others nodded, understanding the weight of his words. But they also knew that not all of them

would make it out alive.

The sun dipped below the horizon, casting long

shadows over the desolate landscape. The air was thick with tension as the group of scientists and soldiers prepared for the final assault on the

asteroid. The compound they had developed—the ultimate version of the Anti-Predator Compound— was their last hope. The plan was simple but

perilous: inject the compound directly into the heart of the asteroid, where the predators' hive mind was centered.

Emily, Hank, Carl, and the others knew the risks.

They had seen the predators evolve, adapt, and

grow stronger. They had lost friends and loved ones to these monstrous creatures. Now, it was their

turn to strike back, to end the nightmare once and for all.

Chapter 5

They moved in silence, their faces grim and determined. The predators had decimated the American continent and were advancing rapidly. Time was running out. The group approached the asteroid, its surface glowing with an eerie, otherworldly light. They could feel the power emanating from it, a palpable sense of dread.

" Stay sharp," Hank whispered, his eyes scanning the horizon. " We don' t know what we' re up against."

Carl nodded, clutching his weapon tightly. " We' ve come this far. We can' t turn back now."

As they reached the base of the asteroid, they saw the King Predator. It stood tall, its blue eyes glowing with malevolence. It was unlike anything they had encountered before. The creature was massive, its body covered in metallic scales that shimmered in the fading light. Its claws were long and razor-sharp, its fangs bared in a menacing snarl.

The King Predator let out a deafening roar, shaking the ground beneath their feet. The battle had begun.

Chapter 5

The King Predator lunged forward with a speed that belied its size. The group scattered, barely avoiding the creature's massive claws. Hank fired his

weapon, but the bullets bounced harmlessly off the predator's armor-like scales.

"Keep moving!" Emily shouted, her voice barely audible over the roar of the King Predator. "We need to distract it long enough to inject the

compound!"

The group split into two teams. Emily, her parents, and Carl would make their way to the heart of the

asteroid, while Hank and the others would keep the King Predator occupied. The ground trembled as the creature continued its relentless assault.

Hank ducked under a swipe from the King

Predator's claws, rolling to his feet and firing

another round. "Come on, you ugly bastard!" he

yelled, trying to draw its attention away from the

others. The creature turned its glowing blue eyes on him, a low growl rumbling from its throat.

Chapter 5

Carl led the way toward the center of the asteroid, his heart pounding in his chest. He could hear the sounds of battle behind him, but he forced himself to focus. They had to reach the core and inject the

compound, or everything they had fought for would be lost.

As they moved deeper into the asteroid, the air

grew colder, and the light dimmer. They could feel the presence of the hive mind, a malevolent force that seemed to watch their every move. The path was treacherous, with jagged rocks and unstable

ground.

Emily's father, Dr. James Hawke, stumbled but

quickly regained his footing. "We're almost there," he said, his voice strained. "Keep going!"

They reached the heart of the asteroid, a glowing

chamber pulsating with energy. The hive mind was concentrated here, the source of the predators'

power. Emily could feel its influence, a dark presence pressing against her mind.

Chapter 5

Dr. Lillian Hawke prepared the syringe, her hands shaking. "This is it," she said, looking at her

daughter. "We have to do this together."

Emily nodded, taking a deep breath. "Let's end this."

Meanwhile, outside, the battle raged on. Hank and the others were struggling to hold their ground

against the King Predator. The creature was

relentless, its attacks growing more ferocious by the minute. Hank fired another round, aiming for

the creature's mouth—the only vulnerable spot they had discovered.

The bullet hit its mark, and the King Predator let out a roar of pain. But it was not enough to bring the creature down. It lunged at Hank, who barely managed to dodge out of the way.

"Fall back!" Hank shouted to the others. "We can't keep this up much longer!"

Chapter 5

Carl and Emily's parents worked quickly, injecting the compound into the core of the asteroid. The

chamber glowed brighter, the energy pulsing faster.

They could feel the hive mind reacting, a surge of anger and fear.

Suddenly, the ground shook violently, and the King Predator let out a deafening roar. It knew what they were trying to do, and it was determined to stop

them. The creature turned away from Hank and charged toward the asteroid's heart.

"Hurry!" Emily shouted, her voice echoing in the chamber. "We need to finish this before it gets

here!"

Dr. James Hawke injected the last of the compound, and the chamber pulsed with a blinding light. The

hive mind let out a psychic scream, a wave of pain and fear that nearly overwhelmed them.

Chapter 5

The King Predator burst into the chamber, its eyes glowing with fury. It was too late to stop the

process, but it could still exact its revenge. The

creature lunged at Carl, its claws tearing through his body.

"No!" Emily screamed, firing her weapon at the
creature. But the King Predator was too strong. It
turned its attention to Emily, its eyes glowing with hatred.

Hank and the others burst into the chamber, firing their weapons. The King Predator roared in pain,

but it was not enough to bring the creature down. It lunged at Hank, who stood his ground, firing until

his weapon was empty.

The King Predator struck Hank with its massive claws, sending him crashing into the wall. He

struggled to get up, blood pouring from his wounds.

Chapter 5

"Get out of here!" Hank shouted to the others. "Finish the mission!"

Emily's parents grabbed her, pulling her toward the exit. The chamber was collapsing, the energy from

the hive mind becoming unstable.

Hank stood up, facing the King Predator one last time. "This ends now," he said, his voice filled with determination.

The King Predator lunged at Hank, but he was

ready. He pulled out a grenade, pulling the pin and holding it close to his chest. The creature's claws

tore through his body, but he held on, pressing the grenade against the creature's chest.

"See you in hell," Hank whispered, and the grenade exploded, engulfing them both in a blinding light.

Emily and her parents made it out of the chamber just in time. The asteroid shook violently, the

energy from the hive mind becoming unstable. They ran as fast as they could, the ground collapsing

behind them.

Chapter 5

They reached the surface just as the asteroid

exploded, a massive shockwave tearing through the landscape. The predators let out a psychic scream,

their connection to the hive mind severed. One by one, they fell, their bodies collapsing as the hive mind died.

Emily collapsed to the ground, tears streaming
down her face. They had won, but at a great cost.
Hank, Carl, and so many others had given their lives to end the nightmare.

Dr. James Hawke put his arm around his daughter.
" They didn' t die in vain," he said softly. " They saved us all."

Across the continent, predators convulsed and

collapsed, their connection to the asteroid severed. One by one, they fell, their bodies disintegrating as the compound severed their link to the hive mind. The pulse continued to emanate from the asteroid, spreading across the land, dissolving the predators in a wave of energy that left the earth eerily silent.

Chapter 5

As the dust settled, a group of scientists cautiously approached the impact site, drawn by the sudden

silence. They found Emily lying near the asteroid, barely alive, her body battered and broken. They

carefully lifted her, her eyes fluttering open as she gave a faint smile, her voice a whisper.

"It's done," she murmured, her gaze unfocused. "They're gone."

PREDATORS 119

131

Post-Story Scene

The world was healing, though scars from the invasion remained. Cities lay in ruins, roads were overgrown, and wildlife thrived in places once dominated by humanity. But the human spirit had proven resilient, and civilization was gradually rebuilding.

In a modest laboratory that overlooked a green valley, Emily sat with her parents, Dr. Lillian and Dr. James Hawke. They were older now, marked by the weight of survival and loss, but there was a warmth between them—a hard-won peace.

As they reminisced about their past and those who didn't make it, their memories gravitated toward the sacrifices of Hank, Carl, and the others who had fallen in the final battle.

"Carl and Hank," Dr. Lillian whispered, her eyes distant. "They gave everything to ensure we'd have a future. Without them, the rest of us wouldn't be here today."

Post-Story Scene

Emily nodded, her gaze somber. "They didn't hesitate. Even when the odds were against us, they fought because they believed in what we were doing."

A quiet, respectful silence fell over the room, and Dr. James reached out, squeezing Emily's hand. "We honor them by rebuilding, by not giving up on each other. And by making sure the world they saved thrives."

Emily gave a small, sad smile. "They'd want that."

She felt the familiar ache of loss in her chest but also a sense of purpose. The world they lived in now was one built on sacrifice, one that demanded they carry on.

Far across the world, the sun dipped below the horizon over the Indian Ocean. Under the darkening skies, a single shadow moved through the water, slipping silently beneath the waves.

Post-Story Scene

Unconnected to the hive mind, a predator had survived, evolving independently after it had

severed its link during the chaos of the final battle.

Now it moved toward the shores of the Indian

subcontinent, its senses heightened, its movements calculated.

It was free from the hive, and it had adapted.

As it slinked closer to land, the creature' s eyes gleamed—a new, unsettling intelligence stirring within. It moved with purpose, a reminder that

humanity's fight for survival was far from over……

Don't miss out!

Visit the website below and you can sign up to receive emails whenever The Samurai X publishes a new book. There's no charge and no obligation.

https://books2read.com/r/B-A-DNAQC-IERDF

BOOKS 2 READ

Connecting independent readers to independent writers.

www.ingramcontent.com/pod-product-compliance
Ingram Content Group UK Ltd.
Pitfield, Milton Keynes, MK11 3LW, UK
UKHW040659100725
6823UKWH00019B/77